HIPHOP
and His Famous Face

◆ ◆ ◆

Gary J. Oliver
with **H. Norman Wright**
Illustrated by Sharon Dahl

ChariotVICTOR
PUBLISHING
A DIVISION OF COOK COMMUNICATIONS

Everybody knew that HipHop was a funny bunny—the funniest in the forest. And he wanted to stay the funniest. Each day he practiced his funny faces by the pond: wiggling his ears, bugging out his eyes, puffing his cheeks. He made silly faces. Wild and crazy faces. Wacky faces. HipHop's famous funny faces made his friends smile and laugh.

Except for one face that he just couldn't stop—even when he wanted to. When HipHop got really angry, his face wasn't funny anymore. Sometimes HipHop's angry face would even scare his friends away.

One lovely spring day HipHop went looking for his friends. He hoped that no matter what happened, he would be able to keep his angry face hidden away. He wanted his friends to like him, and not be scared off by his anger.

As he hopped down the tree-lined path, he saw his friends Carla Coyote, Elwood Elk, and Bruce Moose standing in the meadow. "Good morning," HipHop said in a cheery voice. "What are you doing?"

Carla answered, "This morning we can't decide what we want to do."

"Do you want to chase butterflies with me?" HipHop asked.

"Chase butterflies?" asked Elwood. "You've got to be kidding. I'm no good at chasing butterflies."

HipHop felt frustrated, but he didn't want his friends to know. So he stuffed his anger inside. But he could still feel it. And when he did this, his eyes got all squinty.

"**W**hat about hide and seek," suggested HipHop.
"I hate that game," complained Bruce. "I always lose."

This time HipHop stomped his foot in anger, but he didn't tell
Bruce what he was feeling. And now not only were his eyes still
squinty, but the insides of his ears suddenly turned bright red.

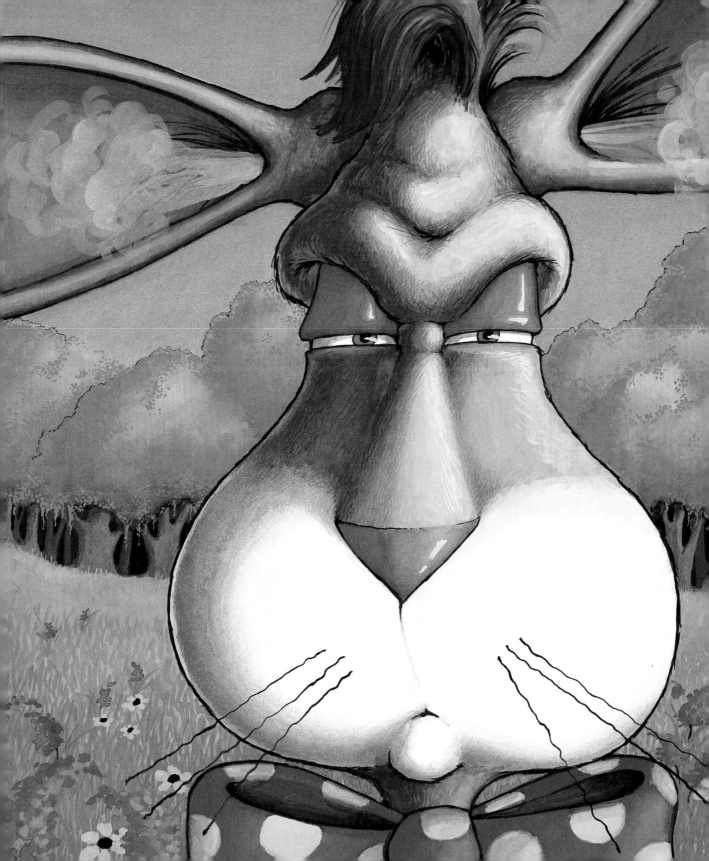

Finally, with a pouty kind of voice, HipHop said, "How about all of us racing to the pond?"

No one was surprised when Carla Coyote said, "Let's go!"

Off they ran just as fast as their paws and hooves would take them. Up the hill, across another meadow, and down the shortcut through the trees. And who got there first? Carla Coyote, of course.

When HipHop saw that Carla had beaten him, he got very, very angry. His eyes were still squinty; his ears were bright red. Next, his hair stood on end. In a loud voice he snapped, "You guys are no fun and I don't want to play with you any more!"

Bruce Moose replied, "HipHop, you're our friend. And you are the funniest bunny in the forest. But when you stuff and stomp and snap, you change. And then we don't like to be with you."

With that, Bruce and Elwood and Carla walked away.

"Well, I never liked them anyway," HipHop mumbled. "I'll go to my secret place and play by myself."

He stomped down the trail, slid down a grassy slope, climbed over a small hill, crawled through a tree stump, and finally came to his secret place. It was a little clearing in the middle of a clump of trees and bushes. A small pool of water stood in the middle. When he felt like nobody liked him, when he didn't understand his feelings, when he wanted to feel safe, HipHop would go to this secret place.

HipHop sat down next to the little pool. He thought to himself, "Nobody will be able to find me here." So he sat and he sat. There was no one to make him frustrated, or hurt, or sad. But there was nobody to talk to either. He thought he would feel better, but he didn't. He felt lonely.

Suddenly he heard a funny noise. He looked around, but he didn't see anyone.

He heard the noise again.

He looked up just in time to see Brenda Blue Jay land next to him.

"Is that you, HipHop? You looked so different, I almost didn't recognize you," she said.

"What do you mean—different?" he asked gruffly.

"Well, take a look at yourself," said Brenda.

HipHop checked his reflection in the pool. No wonder Brenda didn't recognize him! Instead of the funniest bunny in the forest, he had become the ugliest bunny. His eyes were squinty, his ears were red, and his hair stood on end. As soon as he saw his reflection, his angry face became a very sad face.

"**W**hat are you doing here alone?" Brenda asked.

"Just having fun by myself."

"If you're having so much fun, why do you look and sound so sad?"

"I'm angry and I want to be alone," HipHop replied.

Brenda looked deep into HipHop's sad eyes and said, "Sometimes when we get hurt or feel frustrated, we get angry. And sometimes if we sit on our anger, it can become red hot. And when we let our anger get red hot, we can do or say things that hurt people."

"What do you do when you feel red-hot anger?" asked HipHop.

"My feelings don't get red hot very often."

HipHop was surprised to hear Brenda say that. He thought everyone felt things the same way he did. "Why don't your feelings get red hot very often?" he asked.

"Because," said Brenda, "when I start to get angry, I've learned to talk about what I'm feeling."

HipHop replied, "When I get angry, I stuff and stomp and snap."

Brenda began to clean her feathers. Then she asked, "Does it help to stuff and stomp and snap?"

"It doesn't," HipHop admitted.

"And how do you feel when your friends don't like you?"

"I feel hurt and sad. And then I feel mad."

"So, sometimes when you feel mad, it's because you first felt hurt and sad?" Brenda asked.

"I guess so," said HipHop. "I had never thought of that."

"Well," said Brenda—in that matter-of-fact way that Blue Jays sometimes have—"if stuffing, stomping, and snapping don't help, what else could you do that might work better?"

HipHop didn't know how to answer.

As Brenda started to fly away, she said, "Next time you want to stuff and stomp and snap, tell your friends what you feel, and see if that helps."

The next day, HipHop was on his way to the pond to chase butterflies when he saw his friends playing in the meadow. Elwood, Bruce, and Carla had been joined by Ric and Rac and Buford. He hopped over and hoped they would invite him to play. But they didn't. And it hurt. HipHop felt sad.

When Elwood saw that he was sad, and not mad, he said, "HipHop, would you like to play with us?"

"Sure," said HipHop. But as he ran over to join his friends, he tripped over a rock and rolled on the ground. When he got up, he could feel the mud sticking to his face. He heard his friends start to snicker. Then they laughed even louder.

HipHop was embarrassed that he had fallen in the mud. He didn't like his friends laughing at him. He felt his eyes getting squinty and his ears getting red. He knew what that meant!

"It's not funny," HipHop snapped. "It doesn't feel good to be laughed at!"

"We're not making fun of you," Bruce replied. "We just thought you were trying to be funny. You know, with one of your famous faces."

As soon as he saw his reflection in Elwood's sunglasses, HipHop realized how funny he looked. And he knew why everyone was laughing. HipHop started to laugh himself. "I guess I do look pretty funny." It felt good to laugh instead of stomping and snapping.

Then he tried out a few new funny faces. His friends laughed even louder, and even made some funny faces of their own. But everyone agreed that HipHop—with his famous face—was the funniest in the forest.

GROWING ON:
HOW GROWNUPS CAN HELP A CHILD COPE WITH ANGER

Ask your child to give you his or her definition of anger. Ask: *Do you think anger is good or bad? Where did you learn that?*

Explain that anger is a God–given emotion which everyone experiences. There are different ways to express the anger that all of us experience. Some ways are helpful and some do harm.

Talk about these questions:

★ How did HipHop respond when Elwood Elk didn't want to chase butterflies? Did it make things any better?

☾ How did HipHop respond when Bruce Moose didn't want to play hide and seek? Did it make things any better?

★ What did HipHop do when Carla Coyote beat him to the pond? Did it make things any better?

☾ How did HipHop feel after he let his anger control him?

★ How do you know when mom and dad are angry? What do they look like? How do they sound? Do they ever stuff and stomp and snap? (Spend some time talking with your children about what it means to stuff and stomp and snap. Share examples from your own life that they can relate to.)

☾ How do you know when you are angry? What do you look like? How do you sound? Do you ever stuff and stomp and snap? Does it help?

★ What did HipHop learn from Brenda Blue Jay? (He learned that stuffing and stomping and snapping doesn't help. He learned that underneath his anger are other emotions. He learned that it is important to share what you are really feeling.)